Book Two

of the

by A. J. Atlas
illustrated by Anne Zimanski

Welcome, Readers!

Before you get started, I thought you might like to know a few interesting things about the *Travels with Zozo...™* series. First of all, the stories are set in real places, so the illustrations you'll see try to show the actual landscapes, plants, and animals found in those locations. Second, the cultural and historical elements you'll read about are also as accurate as possible. I hope this knowledge makes the books even more enjoyable for you.

For this story, the settings are in the Scandinavian country of Norway, including the towns of Laerdal, Aurland, and Sogndal (the site of the double trampoline park) and the fjords of Geirangerfjord, Naeroyfjord, and Aurlandsfjord.

In a few parts of the story, a teeny bit more creativity and imagination was added. Most of it will be quite obvious, like the bicycling foxes. (And that funny flat tire!) Other, less obvious, elements that are not 100% accurate include the following:

- Although the illustration of the town of Aurland, near the tunnel entrance, is generally accurate, the nearby, historic Borgund Stave Church is shown in the center of town in place of the local church.
- Sea eagles should not be approached, even though Zozo does. It is not safe to go near or try to touch unknown animals.

For the most part, the rest of the information I have presented is accurate and, in my opinion, super interesting! Here are a few more fun facts:

- A fjord is a long, narrow, deep inlet of the sea with steep sides or cliffs, formed by a glacier.
- Laerdal Tunnel is the world's longest car tunnel. It takes about twenty minutes to drive from one end to the other. It is 15.23 miles (24.51 kilometers) long and connects the towns of Laerdal and Aurland. There are longer tunnels for trains and subways, but not for cars.
- White-tailed sea eagles prefer to grab fish by plucking them out of the water without getting their feathers wet. If they catch a really big fish, however, they have been known to use their wings to row or swim it to shore.

And one last thing, three words with pronunciations that might be new to you include:
- Mikkel — mi-KELL
- Fjord — fee-YOUR-duh
- Laerdal — LAIR-dul

— AJA

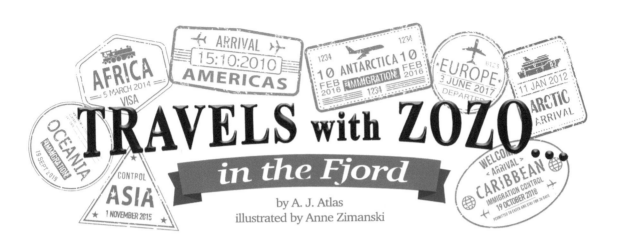

TRAVELS with ZOZO

in the Fjord

by A. J. Atlas

illustrated by Anne Zimanski

IMAGINON
BOOKS

Zozo was a hoppity, floppity, huggable,
snuggable pet bunny who loved to sleep.

She lived with a fun, on-the-run family of four who loved to travel. Together, they crisscrossed the world sharing adventures and making new friends.

Bong

Zozo and her family were on vacation in Norway. The air smelled crisp and clean, and the outdoor park had a double trampoline.

Dad, Mom, Benji, Jazz, and Zozo took turns somersaulting through the air. When Zozo took her turn, she launched herself with all her might from one trampoline to the next and back again. *Bing, bong, boing!*

"Zozo is the world's best trampoline bouncer!"
Zozo's sister, Jazz, cheered.

Zozo blushed. She knew Jazz was joking, but she
had tried to make her turn the best ever.

Jazz always inspired Zozo to try her hardest to be
the best she could be. It was because Jazz herself
liked to be the best at everything she tried.

As the family headed back to their rented vacation home, Zozo remembered how Jazz even wanted to have the best name. She liked her first name, Marie, only a little. Her middle name was Jasmine. She liked that more. But by shortening it to *Jazz*, she felt now she had the best name ever!

Once inside, Zozo hopped eagerly into her comfy bed, happy to rest her tired muscles.

"It looks like we all could use a nap after the fun we had!" Dad said with a yawn. Everyone nodded and set off toward their bedrooms.

From her bed, Zozo took one last, lazy look at the beautiful, green scenery in the backyard. Out of the corner of her eye, she noticed one of their beach towels on the clothesline outside begin to shake. It fell from the line and then quickly moved away. Beneath it, Zozo could see a mass of feathers. A bird was stealing their towel!

"That's not yours!" Zozo yelled, after squirming out of her blanket and bounding out the door. "Put that down!" she shouted, racing across the yard toward the thief.

A white-tailed sea eagle peered out from beneath the towel. "Terribly sorry, little one, we only wanted to borrow it," he said.

Zozo saw another sea eagle in the water sitting on something large. Drawing nearer, Zozo declared, "That towel belongs to my family!"

"Our apologies. I'm Mikkel, and that's Hanna," Mikkel said, pointing to the swimming eagle. "We are bringing food to our babies. May we borrow your towel?"

Zozo followed Mikkel to the water's edge, where Hanna began explaining. "We swam this big fish to shore, but we're very tired now. With the towel," she said, looking kindly at Zozo, "we can carry it between us and fly home."

"Alright," Zozo agreed, happy to help the struggling parents with their difficult task.

Mikkel and Hanna rolled the fish in the towel, and each grabbed an end. "Would you like to come along with us and see more of Norway?" Hanna asked. "You could meet our babies, and we promise to bring you right back."

Zozo had never ridden on a bird. She had ridden in her brother's and sister's arms many times. Once, she had ridden on a bear down a river. She liked rides. *How different could riding a bird be?* she wondered.

"A ride sounds like fun." Zozo finally decided and climbed onto Mikkel's shoulders.

Cool wind blew through Zozo's fur as they
lifted up into the sky. Mikkel and Hanna
flapped their strong wings only a few times,
and then they glided silently for a long while.

"Amazing!" Zozo said, soaring peacefully past
an icy glacier and over the glistening water of the
deep fjord. "Everything is so beautiful. This just
might be the world's best ride!"

The eagles' nest was perched high on a cliff. Mikkel and Hanna landed softly. Then Hanna introduced Zozo. Pointing to the first baby and then the next two, Hannah said, "These are our hungry, little babies. We call them Very Hungry, Super Hungry, and Always Hungry, or for short, Vee, Su, and Al." Everyone giggled.

The sea eagle family ate the big fish quickly. Afterwards, Zozo played with Vee, Su, and Al. She showed them how high she could jump, and the three birds joined in the fun. Meanwhile, Hanna rolled up the towel and prepared to take Zozo home.

Without warning, Al hopped to the edge of the nest and declared, "I'm ready to take my first flight!"

In a blink, he was gone.

Rushing to the edge, Vee, Su, and Zozo looked over. Al was falling along the cliff. Not flying yet, just falling.

"Oh no!" cried Vee.

"Why isn't he flapping his wings? He'll get hurt!" worried Su.

Hanna dropped the towel and flew out of the nest. Mikkel dove off too. Quickly, both parents plunged past Al and then leveled off to glide below him. They were ready to catch him if he didn't start flapping his wings soon.

Al looked surprised and scared. The air rushing past him made it hard to move, and he struggled to flap his wings.

Gradually, he raised his head and looked out at the snowy mountaintops, as if imagining himself soaring over them.

Slowly, Al began flapping his wings.

He stopped falling and flew upwards a little. Using all his strength, he pushed harder.

His wings started moving him higher and higher into the sky. He was flying!

Everyone cheered.

"Look at him go!" Zozo hollered joyfully.

Then Vee and Su looked
at each other, smiled...
and jumped out too.

At first, Vee and Su also
had trouble flapping
their wings.

But looking up toward
the mountaintops and
pushing with all their
might, they stopped
falling and began flying.

"Hurray! Keep going!" Zozo encouraged her new friends. She was proud of the hardworking baby birds. They'd done their very best and had learned to fly. They made her think of Jazz, and Zozo realized she had been gone a long time and needed to hurry home.

"Goodbye," said the sea eagle family, sharing hugs with Zozo before she climbed onto Hanna to fly home.

Hanna had a towel in her talons, Zozo on her shoulders, and an idea.

"It's a long flight back to your house if we travel along the fjord. How about a short cut?" Hanna asked, turning away from the water and toward a small town.

"Sure!" Zozo agreed, curious to see what Hanna had in mind.

As they flew closer, Hanna aimed for a black hole
in the mountainside. Zozo saw it was a tunnel.

Hanna and Zozo flew through the tunnel.
Most of it was long and narrow.

In some parts, the tunnel widened out and looked like a big cave.

"This is the longest tunnel in the world!" Hanna said proudly.

"Wow! A lot of people must have worked very hard to make this," Zozo said, continuing to be impressed mile after mile.

Soon, Zozo was back at her family's vacation home. She
hugged Hanna and thanked her for all the fun. Then,
as Hanna flew away, Zozo slipped inside. Seeing no one
awake and thinking she still had time for a well-deserved
nap, Zozo crawled into bed and closed her eyes.

Pictures of the fun she'd had that day floated through her mind. The day had been full of *bests*. She'd seen the best tunnel. *Well, maybe not the best, but certainly the longest,* she thought.

She'd taken the best ride over the fjord. And she'd been the best trampoline bouncer, at least according to Jazz. As she drifted off to sleep, Zozo was sure of one other best she had. She had the best family. She was absolutely certain of that. They were the best because they were hers.

Discover Australia's Great Barrier Reef in Zozo's next adventure, Travels with Zozo... on the Reef!

Travels with Zozo...in the Fjord   by A.J. Atlas   illustrated by Anne Zimanski

Published by ImaginOn Books,
an imprint of ImaginOn LLC
www.imaginonbooks.com

Copyright © 2022
by A.J. Atlas

1st Edition
2 4 6 8 10 9 7 5 3 1

Printed
in U.S.A.

978-1-954405-02-8 (Hardcover)   978-1-954405-32-5 (Ebook)

To purchase books or obtain more information about the author, illustrator, or upcoming books, visit www.travelswithzozo.com

CPSIA information can be obtained
at www.ICGtesting.com
Printed in the USA
LVHW050230301021
701739LV00004B/29